# ON MOTHER'S LAP

Clarion Books
a Houghton Mifflin Company imprint
215 Park Avenue South, New York, NY 10003
Text copyright © 1972 by Ann Herbert Scott
Illustrations copyright © 1992 by Glo Coalson
Published by arrangement with McGraw-Hill Book Company, New York

For information about this and other Houghton Mifflin trade and reference books
and multimedia products, visit The Bookstore at Houghton Mifflin on the World Wide Web
at (http://www.hmco.com/trade/).

Printed in the U.S.A.

**Library of Congress Cataloging-in-Publication Data**

Scott, Ann Herbert.
On Mother's lap / by Ann Herbert Scott ; illustrated by Glo Coalson.
p.    cm.
Summary: A small Eskimo boy discovers that Mother's lap is a very special place with room
for everyone.
ISBN 0-395-58920-7    PA ISBN 0-395-62976-4
[1. Eskimos—Fiction.  **2.**  Indians of North America—Fiction.]  I. Coalson, Glo, ill.  II. Title.
PZ7.S415On    1992    91-17765
[E]—dc20    CIP    AC

WOZ  10  9  8

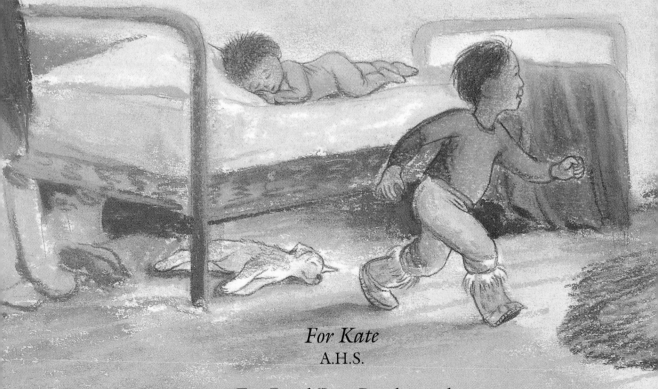

*For Kate*
A.H.S.

*For Jewel Ross Bowles and
LaVerne Bowles Coalson*
G.C.

# ON MOTHER'S LAP

By Ann Herbert Scott

Illustrated by Glo Coalson

*Clarion Books*

New York

Michael was sitting on his mother's lap.
Back and forth,
back and forth, they rocked.

"Let's get Dolly," said Michael.

Soon Michael and Dolly were
on Mother's lap. Back and forth,
back and forth, they rocked.

"Boat needs me," said Michael.
"I'll bring Boat."

Michael climbed back on Mother's lap with Boat on one side and Dolly on the other.

Back and forth, back and forth, they rocked.

13

"I want my reindeer blanket," said Michael.

Carefully, Michael tucked his reindeer
blanket around Boat and Dolly.

Back and forth, back and forth, they
all rocked on Mother's lap.

17

"Puppy wants to come, too," said Michael.

Michael and Boat and Dolly and Puppy
all cuddled beneath the reindeer blanket
on Mother's lap.

Back and forth, back and forth, they
rocked.

"I hear Baby crying," said Mother.
"She'd like to rock, too."

"There isn't room," said Michael.

"Let's see," said Mother.

Michael and Baby both snuggled close
to Mother. Boat and Dolly and Puppy
were in Michael's arms, the reindeer
blanket wrapped around them all.
Back and forth, back and forth, they
rocked.

"It feels good," said Michael.

His mother gave him a squeeze.
"You know, it's a funny thing," she whispered,
"but there is always room on Mother's lap."